fantastic
FRANKIE

For Finley and Ellis
Always be "you" in whatever you do;
no 'you' is better than the 'you' you are.
—J R

American edition published in 2023
by New Frontier Publishing Europe Ltd
www.newfrontierpublishing.us

First published in Great Britain 2022
by New Frontier Publishing Europe Ltd,
Vicarage House, 58-60 Kensington Church Street, London W8 4DB
www.newfrontierpublishing.co.uk

Text and illustrations copyright © 2022 Jessica Rose

The moral rights of the author/illustrator have been asserted.
All rights reserved.

Distributed in the United States and Canada by Lerner Publishing Group Inc.
241 First Avenue North, Minneapolis, MN 55401 USA
www.lernerbooks.com

This book is sold subject to the condition that it shall not, by way of trade or otherwise, be lent, hired out or otherwise circulated in any form of binding or cover other than that in which it is published. No part of this publication may be reproduced, stored in a retrieval system, or transmitted, in any form or by any means (electronic, mechanical, photocopying, recording or otherwise), without the prior written permission of New Frontier Publishing Europe Ltd.

Library of Congress Cataloging-in-Publication data is available.

ISBN: 978-1-915167-33-0

Edited by Tasha Evans · Designed by Verity Clark

Printed in China

10 9 8 7 6 5 4 3 2 1

fantastic FRANKIE

BY JESS ROSE

NEW FRONTIER PUBLISHING

Frankie LOVES *hats,*

Frankie has an **outfit** for *every* occasion.

Frankie *always* stands out.

"WHY IS FRANKIE ALWAYS DRESSED DIFFERENTLY FROM US?"

"WOW!"

"That's better," says Frankie.

"Where is your feather hat, Frankie?" asks Mommy. Frankie says nothing.

"And, where are your favorite sparkly shoes?" pipes up Grandad.

"I don't like them anymore," says Frankie.

"I hate them!" shouts Frankie.

"I HATE hats and shoes, and I HATE SPARKLES!"

"Can I borrow one of your rainbow scarves please, Frankie?" asks Amelia.
"I don't wear those anymore," says Frankie.

"Oh," says Amelia. "That's a shame. They were SO cool!"

"No fabulous hat today, Frankie?" asks Mr. Bon Bon, when Frankie went to buy some chocolate.

"No," sighs Frankie.

"Oh," says Mr. Bon Bon. "What a pity, they *always* make me smile!"

"Not wearing a cape today, Frankie?" asks Postwoman Penny.

"Not today," mutters Frankie.

"Oh," says Penny. "That's a shame! Who's going to be the local superhero now?"

"Ahh, that's better!" says Frankie.

"There's our superhero!" laughs Postwoman Penny, as Frankie swooshed past!

"Look! I've got a scarf like yours, Frankie! Do you like it?" asks Amelia.

"**I LOVE IT!**" whoops Frankie.

Frankie is a **FOX** with plenty of *style* . . .

and that's just the way *Frankie* likes it!